To
Rebecca, Hannah,
Laura, Angie,
& Joseph,

Christmas
FOR A DOLLAR

WRITTEN BY **GALE SEARS**

ILLUSTRATIONS BY **BEN SOWARDS**

Christmas Peace!

Gale Sears

This book is dedicated to my sister-in-law, Nola—a remarkable
artist and a lover of picture books.

—Gale Sears

For Cindy

—Ben Sowards

Text © 2009 Gale Sears
Illustrations © 2009 Ben Sowards

Published by Covenant Communications, Inc.
American Fork, Utah

Printed in Korea
First Printing: October 2009

16 15 14 13 12 11 10 09   10 9 8 7 6 5 4 3 2 1

ISBN-13: 978-1-59811-579-6
ISBN-10: 1-59811-579-0

Christmas
FOR A DOLLAR

WRITTEN BY GALE SEARS

ILLUSTRATIONS BY BEN SOWARDS

Troubles. Eight-year-old Ruthie Kamp threw her hand-me-down jacket aside, thumped the baseball bat on home base, and thought about her troubles.

Thump went the bat. *It's no fun being poor.*

Thump, thump. *I'm tired of thin milk, radish sandwiches, and Depression hash.*

Thump, thump, thump. *I bet Christmas isn't coming again this year.*

A cold November wind stung her face and made her eyes water.

"Oh, stop being a silly goose about Christmas!" Ruthie scolded herself. She looked at her sister Verna on the pitcher's mound in her lightweight dress and worn jacket. Since their mother's death five years ago, Verna had taken on most of the household chores—and she didn't complain. Ruthie looked at her brother Norman smiling from first base. Norman didn't complain about his lot either, though Ruthie thought he had every right.

"Whack it a mile, Ruthie!" Norman called. "If you get me home, we win!"

Norman had been stricken with polio the year their mother died. His left arm was crippled, and his legs were weak, but that never held him back from doing yard work, playing baseball, or pretending to be a hero of the Wild West.

Norman loved books about cowboys and horses, and the last memory Ruthie had of her mama was her soft voice reading Norman off to sleep with Hopalong Cassidy.

Ruthie thumped the bat hard on the base to keep back tears. "Come on, Verna, just try and get it past me!"

Ruthie's other brothers, Russell and Warren, teased her from the outfield.

"Aw, baby sister, you're just a girl!"

"You can't hit it past the pitcher's mound!"

Verna lobbed the ball toward the plate. Ruthie gripped the bat tightly and whacked it! She let out a whoop and started running.

Since it was one-base baseball, she passed Norman as he loped awkwardly toward home. Suddenly, Ruthie heard a thump and grunt behind her. She turned back and saw Norman lying facedown in the dirt. She ran with her brothers and sister to his side.

"Norman, are you all right?" Verna asked anxiously.

Norman grabbed home plate—the welcome mat from the front porch—and struggled to his feet. "What? You've never seen Babe the Great Bambino slide in to home?" He chuckled at the stunned looks his brothers and sisters were giving him. "Ruthie and I win!"

Ruthie cheered, Verna laughed, and Warren and Russell called foul.

Suddenly, Russell looked across the field toward their house. "Hey! That's Dad standing on the porch! He's home early."

The Kamp kids ran for home.

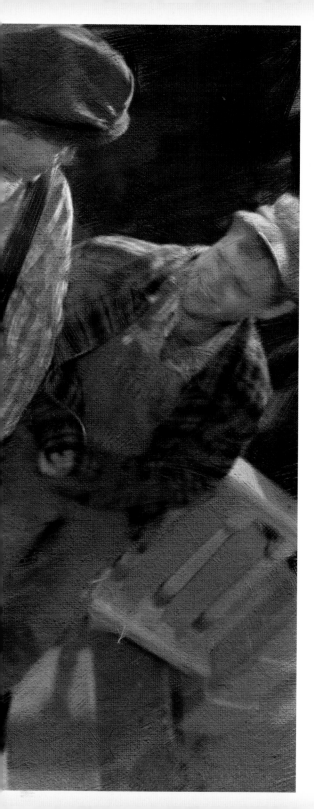

"I'm sorry, Dad. I don't have dinner started," Verna apologized as she approached the porch.

William Kamp smiled and patted his daughter's arm. "You had no idea I'd be home early."

Ruthie ran to her father and threw her arms around his waist. "It's good to see you when the sun's still up."

She didn't care that his clothes were grubby with dirt and grime. She loved her dad, and she knew he worked hard for them. Each day he spent ten to twelve hours in the California oil fields, making barely enough money to put food on the table.

"Miss Ruthie, look who I found waiting for you on the porch." Her father winked at her as he brought her treasured Kewpie doll from behind his back. "Looks like her dress is getting a little worn out."

"Yes, sir," Ruthie answered, giving Kewpie a hug. "But I just tell her what Verna always tells us." Ruthie put on a very grown-up voice. "Use it up, wear it out, make do, or do without."

William Kamp threw back his head and laughed.

A chill wind rustled the leaves in the yard, but Ruthie hardly felt it.

"Let's get in out of the cold," her father said, taking her hand. "And after dinner, I have a surprise for all of you."

When the dishes from supper had been washed and put away, the family gathered in the living room for a family meeting. William held up a tin Band-Aid box and his best Sunday hat turned upside down. He shook the box, and it rattled. "In here I have an idea for Christmas!" he said, smiling at their puzzled looks. He popped open the lid of the box and poured the contents onto the coffee table.

Ruthie could hardly believe her eyes as she stared at the coins winking in the lamplight.

"Man, oh man, Dad!" Warren said. "That's a whole dollar!"

William Kamp laughed as he looked around at his children's astonished faces. "Now I know a dollar is quite a bit of money, but it can only go so far." He picked up his hat from the coffee table. "So, here's what I thought. In my hat are our names on pieces of paper. We'll each choose a name, and then we'll do something special for that person."

"Or make something," Norman said reaching for a name.

His father smiled at him. "Or make something." He picked up a dime. "The coins are here if you need a little money." He looked around at his children. "So, what do you think of the plan?"

Ruthie ran to her father and hugged him. "I think Christmas is coming!"

Over the next few days, coins began disappearing from the little Band-Aid box. Ruthie bubbled with excitement as she took a quarter. She had a special surprise in mind and had asked her father to help her with it.

Little by little, Christmas cheer filled the Kamp home. Warren and Russell decorated a small potted pine tree with their few family ornaments of Danish elves, adding their own handmade paper snowflakes and green-and-red painted clothespins. Verna used a dime to buy a box of thirty Christmas cards, attached each to a green plaid ribbon, and hung them to flutter from the ceiling. When Ruthie saw them, she danced with delight at the special memories they brought back. She had only been three that last Christmas her mother was alive, but she remembered watching her mother and father laugh together as they hung the whimsical holiday decorations.

The only one who seemed to be missing from all the fun was Norman. And Ruthie was worried about him. Almost every day after school he would disappear, dragging into the house just before dinner looking very tired. Ruthie talked to Verna, and they decided to share their worries with their father.

Verna's eyes filled with tears. "He's fragile, Dad, and we wouldn't want to take any chance of the polio coming back."

"Oh, sweetheart," William said softly. "We're all done with that. And Norman is not fragile. He's a tough little man."

"We'd just feel better if we knew he was okay," Ruthie added.

William thought a moment, then nodded. "All right, I'll do some checking."

"Don't let him know!" Ruthie said quickly. "We don't want to ruin his surprise."

William chuckled and hugged his girls. "I'll be very careful."

On his way home from work the next day, William saw Norman coming from Mr. Mueller's fix-it shop. William could see that his youngest son was very tired, as Norman was shuffling along and concentrating hard so he wouldn't fall.

"What in the world could he be working on in a fix-it shop with all the tools, saws, and machines?" William mumbled. "He can't use any of those things with one hand."

When Norman was well out of sight, William walked over and had a talk with Mr. Mueller. A few minutes later he stepped from the store, wiping tears from his eyes. He still didn't know exactly what his son was working on, but Mr. Mueller had told him he'd never seen anyone work so hard or carefully on a project.

The secrets, planning, and excitement continued, and at last, Christmas morning arrived.

Ruthie woke up to a delicious smell. She jumped out of bed, dressed quickly, and ran down to the kitchen, where she found Verna cooking aebleskievers! The round Danish pancake balls had been their mother's specialty.

Ruthie danced about the kitchen with Kewpie, and then they both settled down to help with breakfast. As she set Norman's place, Ruthie felt a little twinge of worry. The night before, Norman had been so tired that he'd fallen asleep at the table, and as William carried him up to bed, Ruthie had noticed blisters on his good hand. She hoped he'd been able to finish his secret gift. She set Norman's knife, fork, and spoon with great care, and placed his glass just so. As she put down his plate, she realized a curious thing—she was more excited about the present she was giving than about the present she would be getting. In fact, she could hardly wait!

The Kamp family sat around the breakfast table eating, laughing, and singing Christmas carols. Ruthie brought the family Bible to her father, and he read the story of the birth of the baby Jesus. Ruthie loved imagining the faraway place in the story, the camels and the Wise Men, and the peculiar gifts. She wished she could see the bright star shining and stand at the side of the baby's cradle. She didn't quite understand the gift of Jesus that her father talked about, but a warm feeling washed over her when she heard the stories of the grown-up Jesus feeding people, taking away their blindness, and comforting them when they were sad.

When William finished reading, Norman moved over to stand close to his father. "Dad, do you think if Jesus was here today, He could heal my crippled arm—make it strong again?"

Ruthie held her breath, wondering what her father would say.

"I'm sure Jesus could heal you, little champ, but I think He gave you another kind of strength—strength of character, strength to help other people." William gave his son a squeeze and then smiled at his other children. "Well, kids, don't you think we've waited long enough for presents?"

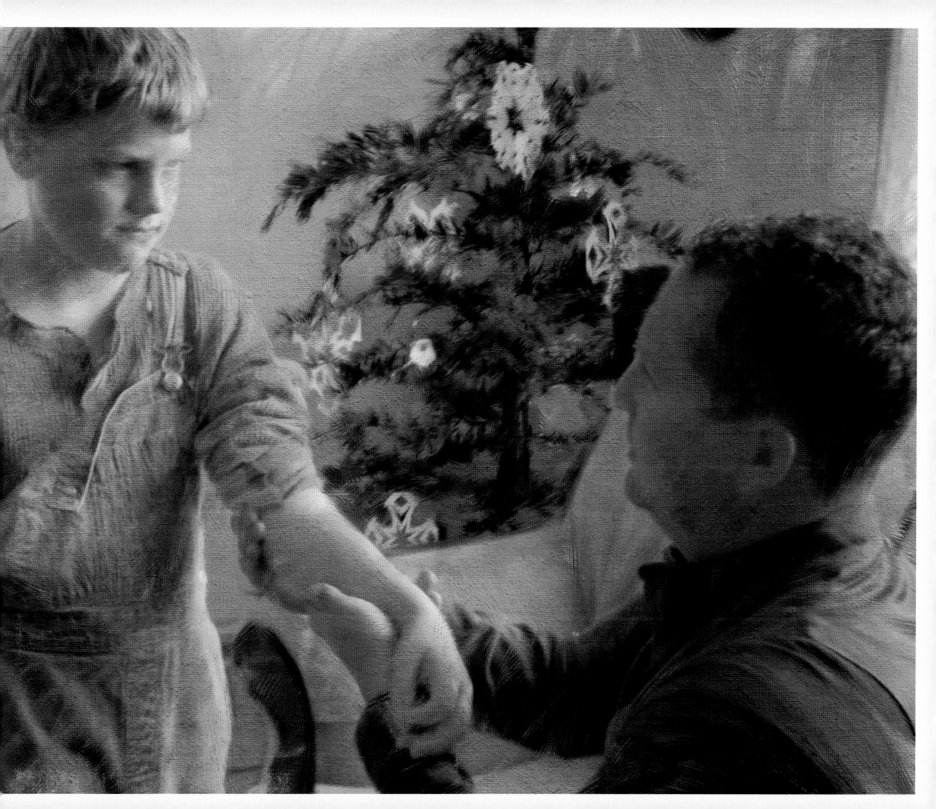

Warren and Russell jostled each other as they raced into the living room.

"If it's okay, I'll go first," Russell said, handing his father a box. "I picked your name, Dad."

Ruthie thought Russell looked nervous as William opened his gift.

"I know you've wanted one," Russell said quickly. "It's not new. Mrs. Lewis was getting a new one, so she gave this one to me."

Their father brought out a Nativity scene with Mary, Joseph, and the baby Jesus.

"There are only two Wise Men," Russell said hesitantly. "And the angel has a cracked wing."

William gently placed the final piece on the table and looked at Russell with misty eyes. "I love it, son. Thank you."

"**I**'m next!" Warren said, handing a box to Russell.

"Watch out!" Norman teased. "It's probably rocks."

Russell's eyes went wide as he opened the box and pulled out Warren's cherished baseball glove. "You're giving me your fielder's glove?"

Warren looked embarrassed by Russell's enthusiasm. "Sure, with my job down at the auto shop, I don't have much time to play anymore."

Russell put on the glove and pretended to catch a high fly ball. "Thanks, Warren. It's swell!"

"Watch your language," Verna said, raising her hand to go next. She handed Warren a beautifully wrapped box.

Warren carefully opened it and pulled out a stack of *Popular Mechanics* magazines.

"Wow, sis! These are great! There must be twenty or more here."

"Well, they're used—I've been collecting them—but with a little of the Christmas money added to some I've been saving, I got you a year's subscription too." She handed him a bright, shiny magazine with his name on the mailing label.

Warren stood to hug his sister as his brothers teased. He ignored them. "What a terrific gift, sis. Thanks."

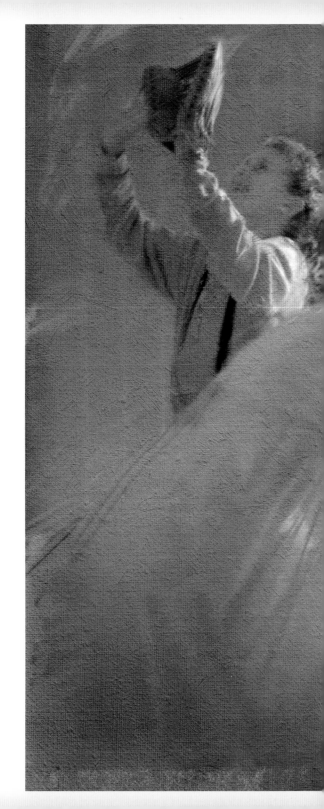

"I think it's your turn, Verna," William said as he drew an envelope from the branches of the Christmas tree."

Ruthie could hardly wait for Verna to open the envelope.

Verna gave her father a curious smile as she drew an official-looking letter out of the envelope. As she read it, her eyes filled with tears. "An application to the junior college?" she whispered. She looked at her father. "Dad, we can't afford this–plus, I don't have the time."

Ruthie jumped up. "But, we're going to help! Dad's going to help with the cooking, I'm doing the dishes, Warren's doing laundry, Russell is cleaning floors–"

"And I'm dusting and polishing!" Norman said proudly.

Ruthie ran over and threw her arms around her sister's waist. "We love you, Verna, and we all want you to be a nurse, if that's what you want to be."

Just then there was a knock at the front door.

"My surprise!" Ruthie said, running to open the door.

On the porch stood their neighbor, Mr. Leamon. "Hi, Ruthie. I brought him, just like we bargained."

The family gathered on the porch, and Ruthie took Norman's hand. "I picked your name, so I got you—"

"A horse?" Russell blurted out, looking at the little pinto pony tied to the front gate.

"Good bargaining," Warren said. "That Christmas money sure went a long way."

"Oh! I didn't buy him!" Ruthie said, stamping her foot. "I rented him for the afternoon." She turned to Norman. "I know how much you like Hopalong Cassidy and all that cowboy stuff."

Norman stared in wonder at the horse. "Can I really ride him, Dad?"

"Can you think of any reason why you can't?"

Norman slowly shook his head. "No."

"Then that's your answer."

Mr. Leamon smiled. "Well, I'll leave you to it then. Here are some chaps and a cowboy hat my boy used to wear when he was young." He shook hands with Norman and turned to walk away. "His name's Pete, and he's as good as they come."

"Thanks for bringing him, Mr. Leamon," Ruthie called.

Norman plopped the cowboy hat onto his head and started off the porch. Suddenly he stopped and turned back. "Hey! Wait a minute! I haven't given Ruthie her present!"

He hurried to his bedroom and was back a moment later, carrying something heavy in his pillowcase. He set it carefully in front of his little sister. Ruthie pushed back the soft cloth of the pillowcase, and Verna gasped. Norman's gift to Ruthie was a handcrafted wooden box—a box he had cut, nailed, sanded, and painted with one hand.

Ruthie knew how hard her brother had worked on the gift—she'd seen him drag into the house every night, and she'd seen the blisters on his hand. Tears trickled down her cheeks, and she didn't even try to wipe them away. She ran her hands lovingly over the smooth wood. "Oh, Norman, thank you. It's the most beautiful present in the world."

"Man, oh man, little brother," Warren said in awe. "You made that?"

Norman nodded.

"Well done, son," William said, laying a hand on Norman's shoulder.

Norman looked around at his family. "It's just a wooden box," he said modestly.

But they all knew better.

Later that day, Ruthie sat contentedly on the porch, playing with her doll. Verna had surprised her with an extra gift—new clothes for Kewpie! Ruthie set Kewpie on her lap and ran her hands over the smooth wood of her new treasure box for the hundredth time.

She heard a whoop and looked up to see her brothers playing in the big field across the street. She giggled when she saw Hopalong Cassidy—Norman—galloping hard after the mangy cattle rustlers—Warren and Russell.

Ruthie put Kewpie and her new clothes inside the treasure box, fastened the top button of her jacket, and went to join her brothers in their game. It had been such a wonderful Christmas. How had it been possible? How had there been enough money for the decorations, food, and wonderful gifts each of them had received? A familiar story itched at the back of her mind—something about fish, bread, and a lot of hungry people. Ruthie smiled. Was this another miracle from the gentle man from Bethlehem—a miracle that had turned a few coins into such a day of joy?

Yes!

Ruthie ran out to the field, and her brothers helped her up onto the pony. She threw her arms around Norman's waist as he urged Pete into a trot, and Hopalong and his gal took off into the sunset, laughing with the abandon of childhood.